Thank you so Much!

Enjoy the book!

Charlie soared through an unfamiliar forest without a worry or a care.
Charlie then saw something unexpected - a big black bear sitting by her large lair.

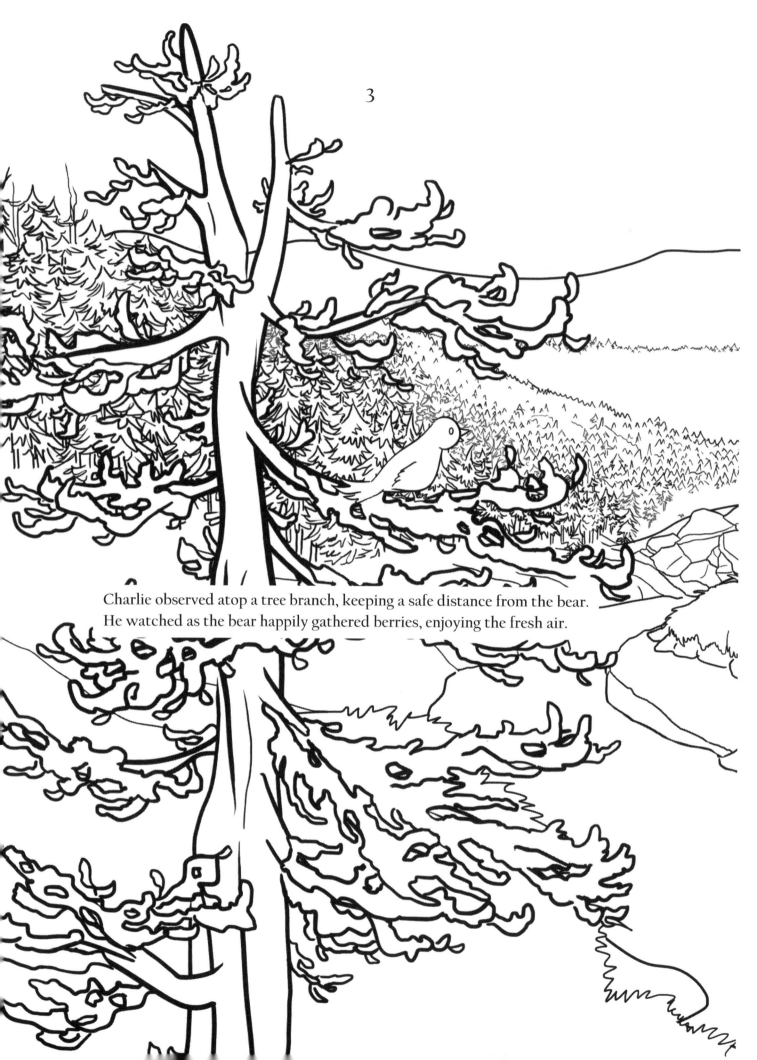

Charlie observed atop a tree branch, keeping a safe distance from the bear.
He watched as the bear happily gathered berries, enjoying the fresh air.

The bear spotted Charlie and smiled. She said, "Hello, bird! What are you doing up in sky so bright?"

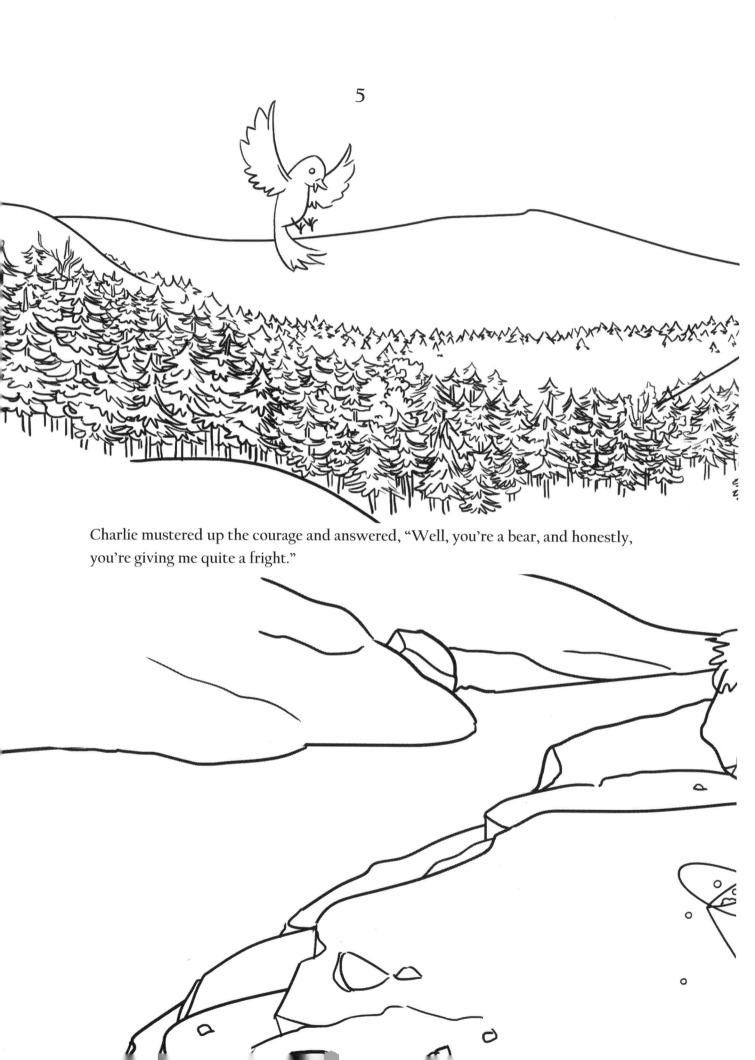

Charlie mustered up the courage and answered, "Well, you're a bear, and honestly, you're giving me quite a fright."

The bear laughed at Charlie's response, which took Charlie by surprise.
The bear laughed so hard that tears flowed from her eyes.

"I'm sorry to have laughed," the bear said calmly, "but I want you to know that you're safe, whether you are down here or up there."

The bear waved her paw and said,

"Hello, my name is Claire. I am a bear, who does not scare."

Charlie frowned.

"That is absurd! There is no way you are a bear who does not scare."

Claire replied,

"Absurd? Do you find it hard to believe that I am a bear who does not scare?"

Charlie continued, "Well, bears are known to scare. That is something they just do."
Claire rubbed her chin. "Really? That's news to me. Can you enlighten me, please?
Because I didn't have a clue."

Charlie explained, "Bears are feared because they are so aggressive with their sharp claws and loud roar. Other animals stay away because they are frightened to their very core!"

"Bears will hunt all animals, both short and tall.
They will hunt them in a flowing river or even up a mountain wall."

Claire remained quiet as Charlie continued, "I wish other animals would take heed and beware, that it is always bad news when one encounters a bear."

Claire smiled, stood up, and silently walked away.
Charlie was confused by her actions. "What is wrong?
What happened? What did I say?"

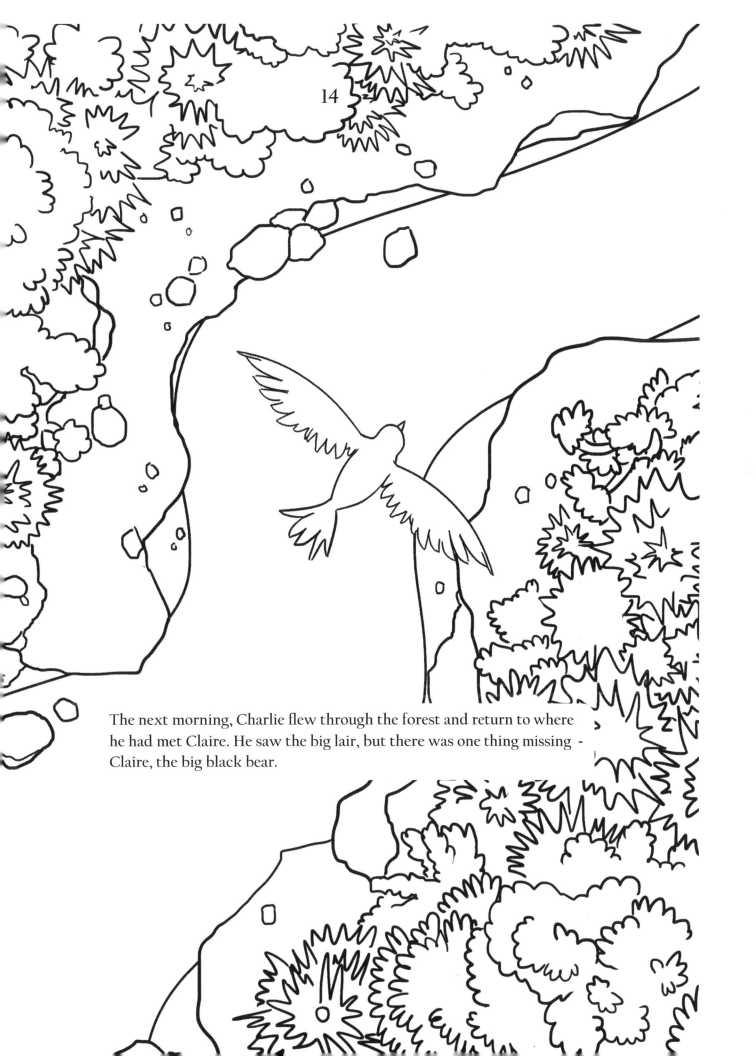

The next morning, Charlie flew through the forest and return to where he had met Claire. He saw the big lair, but there was one thing missing - Claire, the big black bear.

Suddenly, Charlie heard a loud roar and grumble that shook the trees.
The sound was close by.
Charlie panicked. "I knew it!" he cried. "I knew that a bear would attack
the animals of the forest! Why didn't I warn the other animals? Why? Why? Why?"

Charlie followed the sound and was astonished by what he saw.
It was Claire sleeping on a log. She was not attacking any animals at all.

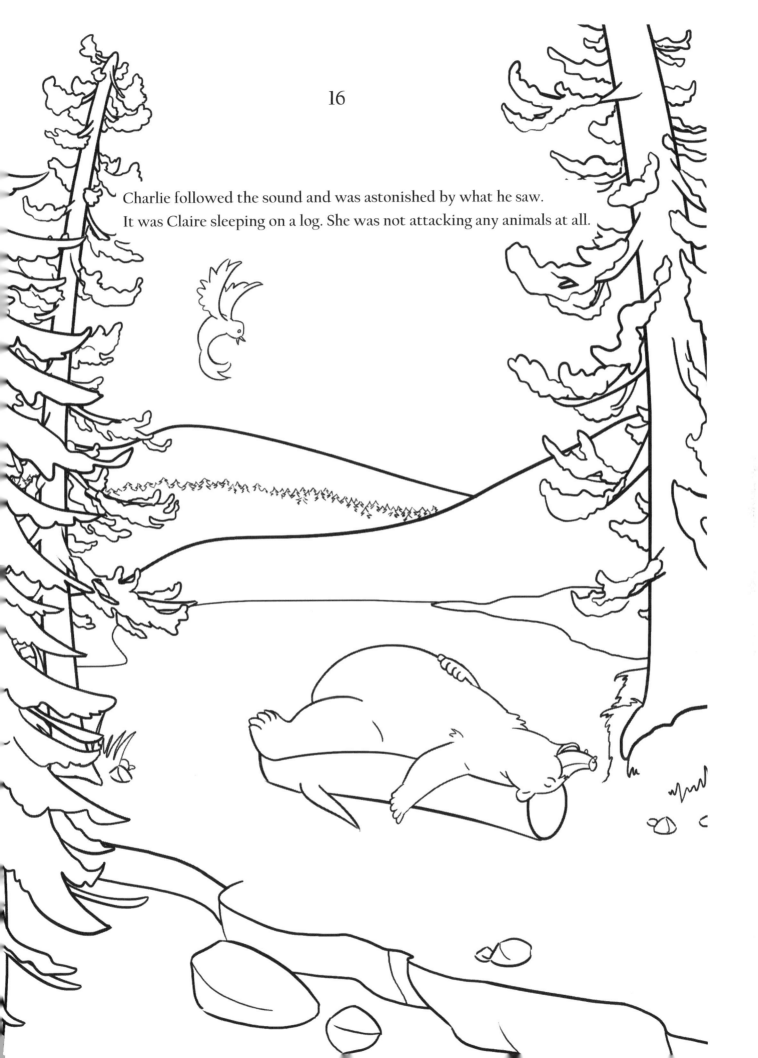

Claire opened her eyes, yawned, and greeted Charlie with a smile. "Hey bird, great to see you again. What brings you here today?" Charlie landed next to Claire and answered, "Yesterday, you just walked away without saying a word, so I wanted to see if everything was okay."

Claire smiled. "Oh, you seemed to have had bad experiences with bears you've met before, and I didn't want to make it any worse."

Charlie felt embarrassed and answered, "Actually, I've never met a real bear - you are my very first."

Claire was amazed. "You've never met a bear before? Then where did all your ideas about bears come from?"
Charlie felt embarrassed and answered, "My ideas came from my dad and mom, and no bears even live in the forest from which I come."

Claire shook her head and replied, "I guess what I've heard
is true about birds, so it makes sense for you to think that way."
Charlie looked puzzled. "For me to think that way?
What does that mean? What are you trying to say?"

Claire shrugged her shoulders, turned around, and began to walk away,
but Charlie flew in her path, ensuring she had to stay.

"You can't leave without explaining why you would say such things about birds," said Charlie. "It's rude to say such hurtful words."

Claire sighed. "Well, I've heard that birds are not too bright
and believe anything they are told. I never met a bird before you,
but I've heard that birds are gullible, whether young or old."

Charlie responded angrily, "How can you say such a thing about birds? Especially when you've never met one?"
A mischievous smirk came across Claire's face. "I don't know," she said thoughtfully. "How can I say such things, especially when I've never met one?"

Charlie paused. Then he understood the lesson that came from Claire.

"I am sorry," he said. "I am sorry for the hurtful words I said to you about bears."

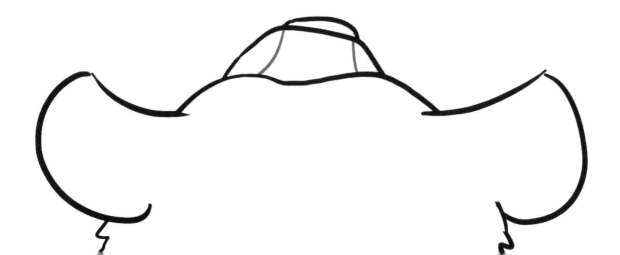

Claire smiled kindly and replied, "Apology accepted with no harm done.
I would like to welcome you to my forest, where all the animals can be safe
and have fun."

Charlie held up his wing and said, "Great! Let me introduce myself,
My name is Charlie the canary. Nice to meet you, Claire the bear."
Claire gently shook Charlie's wing and said, "Hello Charlie, My name is Claire.
I am a bear, who does not scare."

Jeffrey Lee Cheatham II *is an author from Seattle, WA.*

Since 2014, he has self-published three children books,

"The Family Jones and The Eggs of Rex", "Why is Jane so Mad?"

and "Hi Blue Sky" to increase positive representation

of children of color in books.

In 2016, Jeffrey created the Seattle Urban Book Expo,

with the mission of providing a platform for fellow authors

of color to showcase their literary arts in the Pacific Northwest.

For more information visit www.jeffcheatham2.com/author

Made in the USA
Middletown, DE
29 June 2021